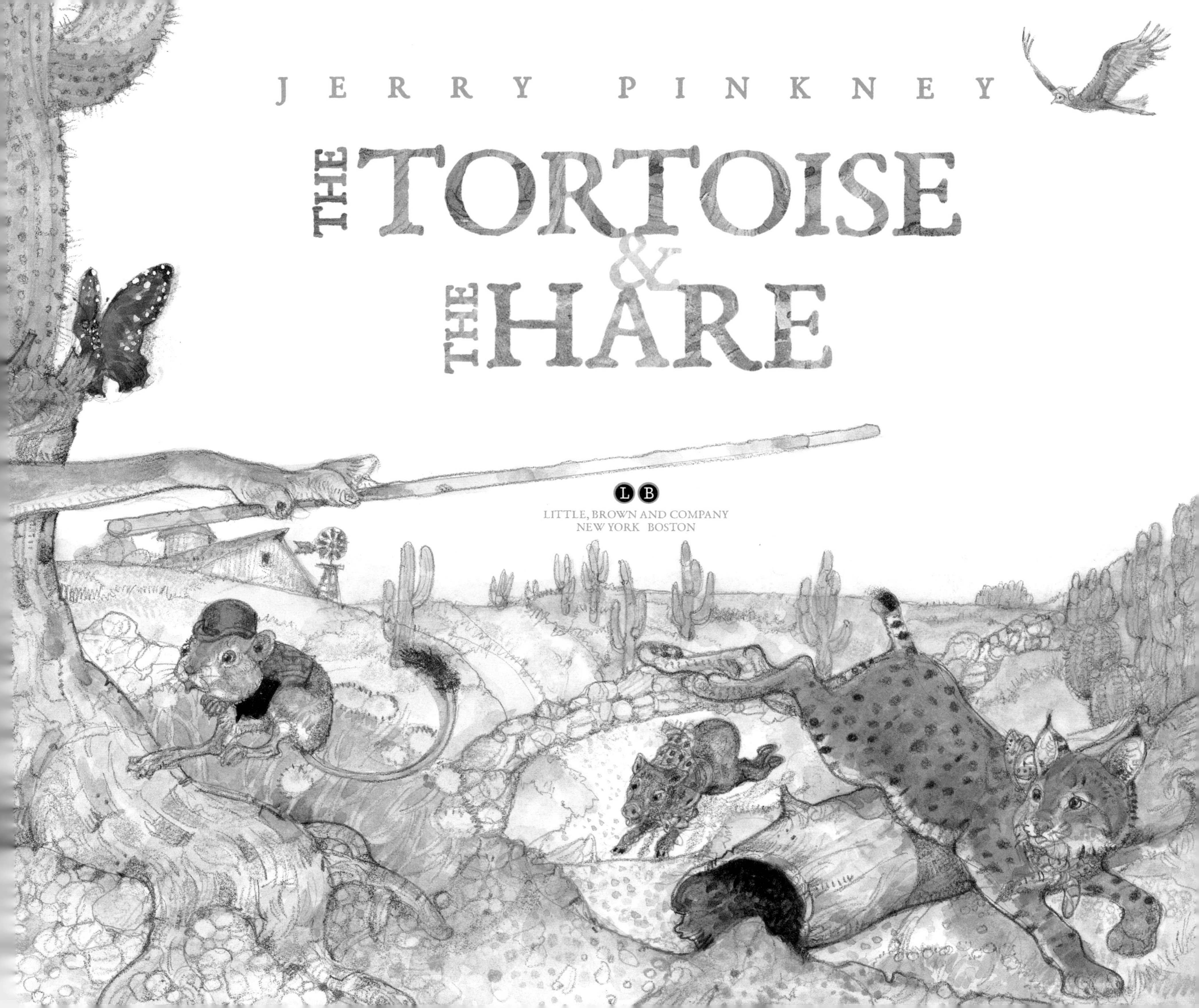

JERRY PINKNEY

THE TORTOISE & THE HARE

LB
LITTLE, BROWN AND COMPANY
NEW YORK BOSTON

On your marks,

get set...

Go!

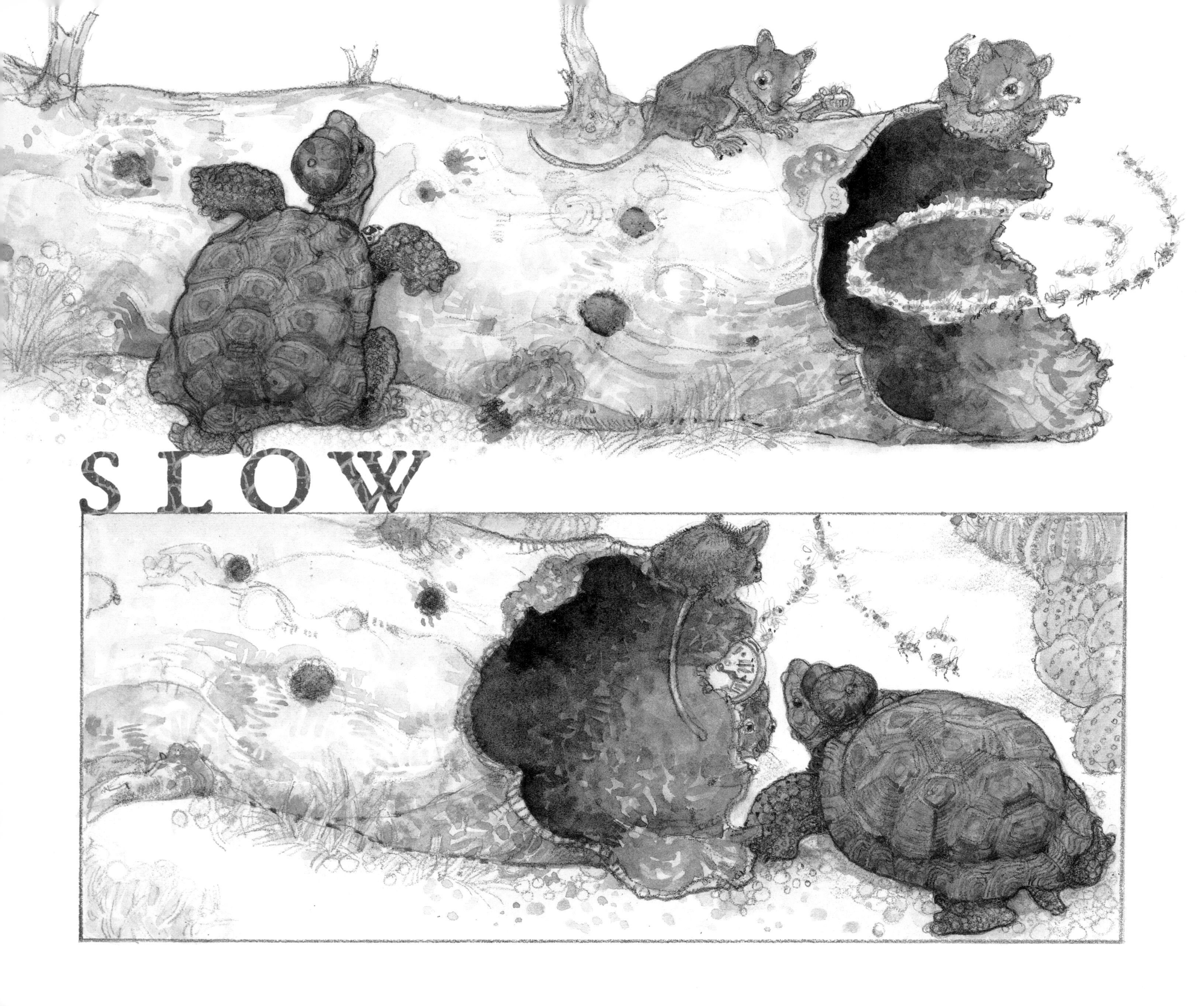
SLOW

SLOW
AND

SLOW AND STEADY

SLOW
AND
STEADY
WINS

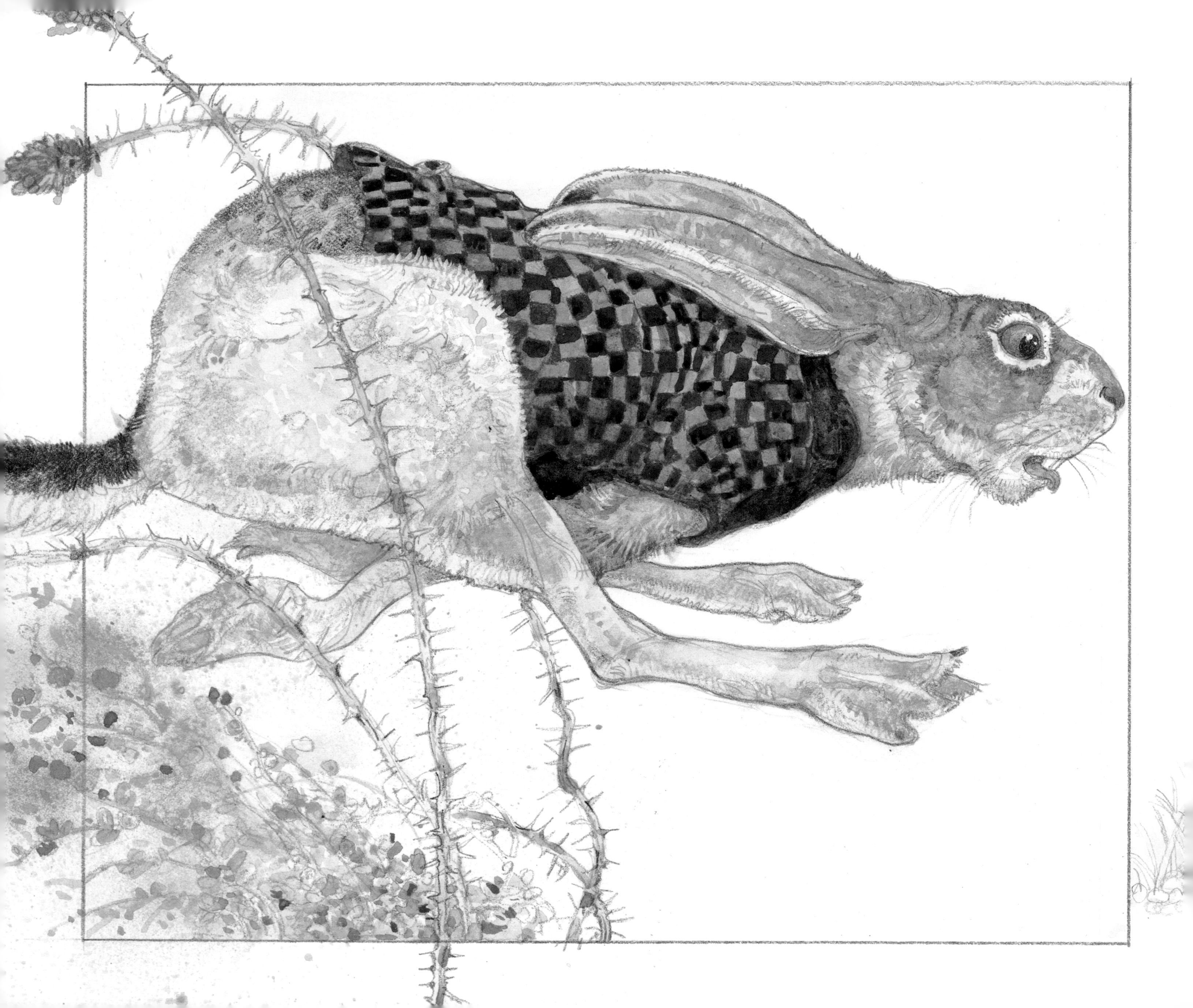

SLOW AND STEADY WINS THE

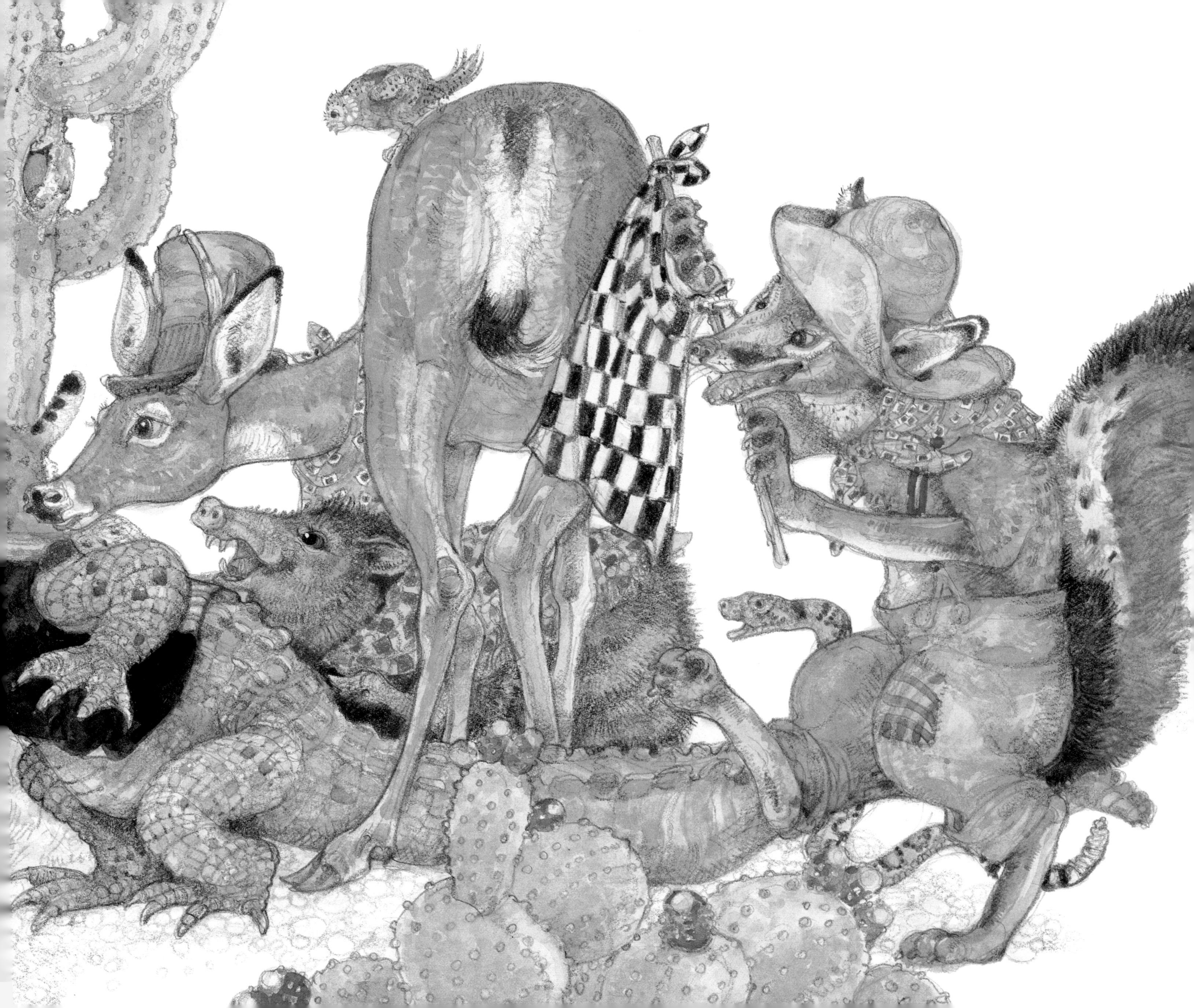

SLOW AND

STEADY WINS THE RACE!

ARTIST'S NOTE

I remember hearing "The Tortoise and the Hare" when I was a child, not just as one of Aesop's classic fables but also as one of the tales of Uncle Remus. In my family, stories such as this were often shared orally, in the same manner that they had been passed down for generations. I have always been intrigued by the fact that this fixture of my own childhood lived also in the imaginations of colonial enslaved people.

"Slow and steady wins the race" was particularly meaningful in my youth, since I often struggled in school because of dyslexia, but the moral rings truer than ever today. As the pace of our lives continues to speed up, many yearn for a less hurried approach to life. The tortoise proves that it can be wise to have a goal, but one should relish the process of getting there. The handling of the text in this version echoes that message by starting over, again and again, building momentum toward the finish line. But I wanted the hare to teach something, too: Winning isn't everything. He surprises his friends by not being the sore loser they might expect. Competitors can also be teammates and friends.

I set the characters in the American Southwest because it's a natural habitat for various tortoise and hare species, but both creatures can be found in most arid places around the world. Many animals in these wide-open areas rely on camouflage to hide from predators, so one of my biggest challenges was to make the pictures vibrant; it was a key motivation for my choice to embellish the animals with clothes. The result was imagery reminiscent of the colors of desert flowers blooming against the subtle tones of dusty earth.

I used graphite, watercolor, colored pencils, gouache, and pastel on Arches hot-pressed watercolor paper to create the artwork. My drawings were particularly influenced by a lifelike metal sculpture of a tortoise and a ceramic hare that I stumbled upon at a pet curiosities shop. Having three-dimensional references enabled me to push the dramatic perspectives and compositions that illustrate the fabled race.

Jerry Pinkney

ABOUT THIS BOOK

This book was edited by Andrea Spooner and designed by Saho Fujii. The production was supervised by Charlotte Veaney, and the production editor was Barbara Bakowski. This book was printed on 140gsm Gold Sun Woodfree paper. The text and the display type were set in 1669 Elzevir.

 • Little, Brown and Company • Hachette Book Group • 237 Park Avenue, New York, NY 10017 • Visit our website at www.lb-kids.com • Little, Brown and Company is a division of Hachette Book Group, Inc. • The Little, Brown name and logo are trademarks of Hachette Book Group, Inc. • The publisher is not responsible for websites (or their content) that are not owned by the publisher. • First Edition: October 2013 • Library of Congress Cataloging-in-Publication Data • Pinkney, Jerry, author, illustrator. • The tortoise & the hare / Jerry Pinkney. — First edition. • pages cm • Summary: Illustrations and minimal text relate the familiar fable of the race between a slow tortoise and a quick but foolish hare. • ISBN 978-0-316-18356-7 • [1. Fables. 2. Folklore.] I. Aesop. II. Hare and the tortoise. English. III. Title. IV. Title: Tortoise and the hare. • PZ8. 2.P456Tor 2013 • 398. 2—dc23 • [E] • 2012048426 • 10 9 8 7 6 5 4 3 2 1 • SC • Printed in China

To Brian and Andrea, and their creative spirit. —J. P.